LIVING
BY THE
NUMBERS

Also by Alexandria Blaelock

SHORT STORY COLLECTIONS
The Histories of Hayward Hall
Lovelorn, Lovestruck and Love at First Sight
Common or Garden Variety Heroes
Case Files of the Wilkinson Detective Agency
Unavoidable Fates
Christmas Travesties
Five Faces of Felicia Clarke
Little Place Called Home
Security Directorate Dossiers v. 1.
Security Directorate Dossiers v. 2.

FICTION
That Love Nonsense
Taipan vs Brown
The Ghost and Ms Cox
Friends Like That
Weaving the Wildwood
Wolf vs Orb

MS BLAELOCK'S BOOKS
Stress Free Dinner Parties
Signature Wardrobe Planning
Holistic Personal Finance
Minimally Viable Housekeeping
Planning a Life Worth Living

PICTURE BOOKS
Australia Felix

SELECTED SHORT STORIES
Alma's Grace
Blood and Bloody Profanity
Cancelled by the Cartel
Dingo Hunting
Honoris Virilis Respectu
Mince Pie Mystery
Remains of Christmas
Susan and the Gangster
The Psychic Detective

LIVING BY THE NUMBERS

A SHORT STORY

ALEXANDRIA BLAELOCK

BlueMere Books AUSTRALIA

MELBOURNE, AUSTRALIA

For permission requests, please contact enquiries@bluemerebooks.com.

Ordering Information:
Discounts are available on quantity purchases. For details, contact orders@bluemerebooks.com.

Living by the Numbers/Alexandria Blaelock
paperback ISBN: 978-1-922744-95-1
digital ISBN: 978-1-922744-96-8

Book Layout © BookDesignTemplates.com
Cover Art © Tatiana Kriuchenkova/Depositphotos

LIVING BY THE NUMBERS

Summer poured a fresh cup of organic fair-trade plunger coffee (full-milk cream and two sugars thanks very much) and took it to the old wooden secretary desk she'd rescued from a Council hard waste collection.

She'd carefully sanded it back and painted it a lovely lavender grey which made it a very peaceful place to work, especially since she'd painted the walls a complimentary soft dove blue.

And followed the *Feng Shui* advice to turn her desk around so her back was to the wall and she had a view of both the door and through her workroom window into the garden.

Currently sparkling where the sun hit the early morning dew.

She'd also filled one of the pigeonholes with a small ceramic scent pot, currently dosed with a pleasantly musky "energy" oil blend. Though today, it wasn't really much help countering the after-effects of a restless night.

She sat on a similarly discovered and recycled, hard wooden chair, softened with a flat cushion she'd covered in a dusky pink rose patterned chintz.

She checked her *Neko* cat Daily Numbers Calendar, and read her personal day number forecast:

4 - You'll need pragmatic and methodical energy today to bring about a secure foundation for your future, but don't be too determined to rely on methods that have worked in the past.

Now that she'd taken her reading, she could start trying to plan out her day.

She took a sip of her coffee and pulled a spiral-bound notebook filled with lined, unbleached, recycled paper from a pigeonhole, and a cute, grey cat topped pen from an old jam jar covered in plum *sakura* blossom washi tape.

The notebook, or more properly books, (she'd been gifted a set of five), had ugly bitumen grey covers. She'd prettied up the current book by gluing an arrangement of dried flowers on it, though she lost some of the flowers every time she used it.

Which was every day.

And why she'd lightly sprayed it with hair spray to make the arrangements a little more secure.

The other four were currently stored in a box of dried lavender and seemed to be taking up the scent nicely.

The flowers were more annoying than she'd expected so she thought arranging kawaii stickers on the next one out of the box might be better.

She opened the book to the first blank page (57 according to the numbers she'd written on the bottom outside corners) and wrote the date at the top.

Her silver bangles clinked as she wrote.

Then she sucked the cat head as she thought about what she was grateful for at that precise moment.

Definitely the bright sunshine streaming through the lightly dressed window, so on the first line under the date, she wrote:

1 - Sunshine.

Then taking a sip of coffee, she thought she might need another if she didn't wake up soon, so on the next line she added:

2 - Coffee.

She heard a small thump as a fat, old, grey cat landed on the windowsill and started purring so loudly and thunderously he drowned out the breakfast radio.

Which was probably for the best.

She'd found him passed out on the doorstep on a stormy day, and taken him to a nearby vet to stitch up his war wounds, but they hadn't been able to save his ear.

Not that it mattered, since she'd found he could still hear the fridge door opening perfectly well. And he wasn't showing any inclination to leave, so she added another item to her short list.

3 - Skye.

After a little more coffee, she left a blank line and carefully copied the daily forecast on the following lines.

Secure future, new methods, she mused, clicking her teeth with the pen cat. What new things could she try, that might bring about a more secure future?

But the kind of secure future she was trying to bring about was another matter.

Was it the safe and sound kind of secure?

Or the locked down tight kind of secure?

The sure thing kind of secure?

Or the buy it now kind of secure?

She left another blank line and wrote:

1 - Change the radio station.

What else?

She'd always been a big list writer, should she abandon list writing and try something new?

But if she didn't write lists, what else could she do?

2 - Research planning methods.

She stood up and walked around the desk, pausing at the window to scratch Skye's head as she looked out, trying to come up with something else.

She'd moved to the City the year before to take up a job in a bank.

A job which had disappeared not long after she'd appeared, more's the pity. And she found herself in the strange position of not being able to afford to go home.

Not that there was much home to go home to given she was the only child of deceased parents. Which was the main reason she was in the City.

And as she was in her late twenties, it was way past time she moved out on her own anyway.

She went back to her desk and wrote her next to-do.

3 - Find a friend.

Not that she was likely to find a friend today given she earned her money as a virtual assistant and rarely ventured outside her house.

But in an excess of positivity, because you never know your luck in the big City, she left it as it was.

The quickest and easiest thing on the list was to find a new radio station, so she went back to the radio and pushed the re-tune button. It zipped through the frequencies and settled on a different one.

Summer cocked her head and listened for a moment.

Not specifically for what was being said, but for the tone of the announcer's voice, and the general vibe that came through the speaker at her.

It was calm, and his tenor voice resonated within her rib cage in a not unpleasant way.

So she pushed the set button, went back to her desk and crossed the first item from her list.

Perfect - making progress already.

Time to get to work.

She laid the notebook on its stand on the left side of her desk, put her work planning calendar and list on her right and pulled her laptop from its niche, and powering it up.

The first order of business; check her email to see what jobs came in overnight.

Nothing urgent, but just as she was about to close her email down, she noticed a sale announcement from her favourite stationery shop, and opened it before reason kicked in.

It was mainly expensive fountain pens and coloured inks, and she was fine for them, but just as she had scrolled almost to the bottom and was about to close it, she noticed "The Change Journal" and clicked the link.

The journal contained templates for different organisation and productivity methods, offering the opportunity to try new techniques in a structured way.

It seemed a little expensive, even on sale.

But she clicked the Buy Now button because at least the pink book would cross number two off her list, and she could move on.

In more or less one easy step.

And in a few days, it would arrive, and she could start playing with it.

Then she crossed number two off her list, shut down the email, and got on with her paid work for a couple of good solid hours.

She put her cream coloured kettle on and paced the kitchen while she waited for it to boil.

Secure future, new methods, find a friend...

When she'd moved to the City, she hadn't given any thought to finding local friends.

And even if she had, she'd have assumed she'd make them easily enough at work. And borrow their friends to make herself a place within their circle somehow.

She hadn't given any thought to how else she might meet people.

Her house was so tiny it didn't really deserve the name house, it was more of a flat above a shop than a house, and it was still connected by a locked door.

It was crammed full of all of her parents' things she couldn't bear to get rid of, which was all of it.

Shipping it to the City had been wasteful in so many ways, but she couldn't even look at any of it at the time.

And she still hadn't opened any of the boxes.

Could she get rid of some of it and clear a room to rent out?

Could she even share her home with someone she didn't know?

Maybe if she made a friend, they could share.

She sat back at her desk, with fresh coffee, and carried on with her work.

Lunchtime came soon enough, and she was about to make herself a sandwich when she suddenly realised the obvious.

If she was going to meet new people and make friends, she had to start leaving the house.

So instead of making a quick sandwich, she grabbed the bag she'd bought at the local market and left the house.

As she walked, she looked at the people she shared the sidewalk with. Some were walking with friends, some alone. Some hurried, some walked slowly looking in shop windows.

They met up, talked, and broke up in a continuous psychedelic swirl of movement that reminded her a little of the ant farm she'd had as a child, up until the ants had escaped.

The funny thing was though, that she recognised many of them from other walks she'd taken around the neighbourhood.

These people either lived or worked nearby, and would easily convert to friends given their proximity.

But the idea of just walking up to one of them and striking up a conversation was terrifying.

Though really, she talked to strangers all the time - at the weekend markets, at the library, now and again when she bought take-out.

The key difference was intention; she'd never intended to take those relationships any further.

So, how did you start a conversation with someone in the hope it might go further?

If her job hadn't disappeared so quickly, there was no doubt she'd talk to her colleagues. They'd discuss movies and TV shows, what they'd done on the weekend, boyfriend troubles.

They'd share personal information.

And as the relationships grew, and they decided they could trust each other, they'd share more and more intimate information.

Probably outside of work - over lunch, dinner, or drinks.

So making friends was partly a matter of being in the right place at the right time and picking the right person.

Moving forward, Summer needed to be open to opportunity.

And when it arrived, ready to invite a stranger for coffee.

Or something.

Easy right?

Then why was it so frightening?

She went into her favourite cafe, which was busy as usual, and ordered lunch. She took her order number, and thought very hard about asking a woman sitting alone if she might share her table.

What was the worst possible thing that could happen?

The woman might say no.

Or maybe yes, they got on well, and she followed Summer home and murdered her.

Summer chickened out and sat at an empty table.

She pretended to look at stuff on her phone for a while, but got bored and decided to watch the people instead.

When her salad came, she ate it piece by piece, stabbing poor defenceless chunks of tomato and cucumber as she berated herself for being a chicken.

She told herself not to be too harsh, this was the first time she'd thought about making a friend, it was bound to be hard.

But it didn't really matter, she was disappointed in herself and it cast a pall over what was otherwise a wild and interesting break from routine.

She finished up and left.

As she got home, she noticed the grey front door looked tired and shabby. The paint was faded and peeling in places.

Was that the way that she appeared to others - tired and shabby?

Though she had to admit that today at least, she *did* feel that way.

She opened the door and was faced by the stairs, currently less than half width because the other half was stacked with boxes of her parents' things.

The visible wall was possibly in worse condition than the door!

As she climbed the stairs, she bumped into the stack a couple of times and was surprised at how claustrophobic it was.

How had she not noticed that before?

Turning the corner into the flat to be confronted by a maze of furniture and even more boxes was confounding.

And even though she knew it was there all along, she wondered where it had come from.

There was barely enough room for herself, let alone a friend. Nothing bigger than Skye was going to fit in there.

How on earth did it get this bad?

And she knew the answer to that question too.

Secure future, new methods, find a friend...

She had to do something about this mess.

She weaved her way through the room and passed into her workroom.

Which was startlingly empty by comparison. Just her desk and chair, a cupboard containing her supplies and topped with a networked device that scanned, printed, and faxed and a bookshelf partially filled with her business records, and some reference books.

Neat, clean and efficient.

Standing in the organised space, looking back out, knowing the rest of the flat was as stuffed as the room she could see, she was ashamed.

And pretty sure her parents hadn't intended her to live like this.

Summer hadn't noticed she'd left the radio on until she heard the presenter say, "if there's something in your life you need to change, this is the time to do it."

And she thought something does have to change. And this really is the time.

So instead of going back to her desk to start work, she reached for the closest box and opened it.

The smell of dust, unwashed body and stale air rose to meet her, and she wondered if opening Tutankhamen's tomb had been a little like that.

The box contained one of her mother's cardigans, unwashed, with pockets full of tissues. She hugged it to her chest, nostalgic, remembering her mother wearing it, and decided to keep it.

But she asked herself what she was going to do with it?

It had been sitting in an unopened box for months - she wasn't going to wear it herself, so did she intend to put it in another box and keep it for years?

What was the point in that?

She had to let it go.

She'd wash it and donate it to charity.

Next was a tangle of jewellery, that took next to no time to choose to donate. Some photos and newspaper clippings she set aside to look at later. And a smooth grey stone.

Summer didn't know where the stone originally came from, but before it reached the box, it had been in the kitchen garden.

She turned it over in her hands a few times, then took it and the papers into her workroom; the stone went in an empty pigeonhole in her desk and the papers in an empty space in the bookshelf.

She put the tissues in the bin, the cardigan in the washing machine on the hand wash cycle, and the jewellery back in the box.

Reluctantly, she put the box in her workroom, loath to clutter the room up.

But it made a tiny space in the flat, and when it was full, she could carry it down to the Cat Haven charity shop and donate it.

She opened a second box, and it took her next to no time to decide it was full of actual rubbish for the bin, and items to donate to charity.

In fact, the box was mostly rubbish, so she brought a big rubbish bag to the boxes and threw it in the bag.

Then she packed the donations in her original box and flattened the box she'd just emptied.

The third box was more or less the same, as was the one after that, and the one after that too.

Five boxes so far, and all she was keeping was a stone and some papers to go through later.

She wondered whether to just donate the rest, but felt she owed it to her parents to at least look at their things, and make conscious decisions about them.

Not to mention disposing of the rubbish herself, so the Cat Haven didn't have to.

She threw the rubbish in the bin, the boxes in the recycling, and then carried the charity box down the street.

Despite the load, she was feeling lighter, and free-er, and she smiled and nodded at people she recognised as she walked.

Some smiled and nodded back, or said "afternoon" as they passed.

And that made her feel even better.

Secure future, new methods, find a friend...

At the charity shop, she stopped to chat with the woman and explained that she was going through her parents' things, and querying whether there were any particular items they wouldn't take.

The conversation lengthened, and they talked about cats and Skye and other things.

The next day, she started following her usual routine.

Her personal day number was 7:

You'll look within for answers, use your intuition to accumulate wisdom and solve mysteries, both spiritual and scientific.

And when she considered her actions for the day, she realised she didn't want to follow her usual routine but wanted to spend more time going through her parents' things.

She quickly checked her work planning calendar and email and decided she could spare the morning to see how far she could get on the boxes.

This time she found more to donate, less to throw out, and more to keep.

Half regretfully, she carried a keep box into her workroom. Though there wasn't much point trying to find places for things when she hadn't finished cleaning out.

Then she carried a box down the street to the charity shop and chatted with the woman whose name was Karen, who offered to come by later with a car to collect the boxes.

Summer was very tempted, but when she thought about letting Karen into the flat in its present crowded condition, decided later might be better.

She said she'd keep bringing down the light stuff, but perhaps Karen could come by in a few days when she had more boxes of heavy stuff to go.

On her way home, she stopped by the cafe to buy a latte and a takeout sandwich for lunch and chat with the girl behind the counter.

When she got home, she took a critical look at the furniture maze, and all at once saw how to rearrange it to separate the pieces she wanted to keep from those she didn't *and* make more space at the same time.

So she did, though the flat wasn't ready to invite people into yet.

While she was at it, she dragged all the unopened boxes up from the stairs and started replacing them with the boxes she'd opened and repacked for donation.

She was reluctant to make a start on her paid work, so she sent all her clients a quick email telling them she had an unexpected family matter to take care of, and this would delay her work for a couple of days.

While she knew there was nothing urgent, she asked them to text her if they couldn't wait, because she had to think about her secure future.

As the sun set in a blaze of red and orange, she ate her soggy lunch and felt her life had turned a corner.

The next day, her personal number was 8.

You'll realistically get down to business today in an efficient and pragmatic way, building something of long-term value.

Having given herself the day off work, she started work with the boxes.

Two days of sorting had improved her efficiency and pragmatism, and she made it through all the boxes.

The bulk of it would be going to the Cat Haven shop, with only a few bits and pieces increasing the keep pile.

And as she was in the head space of cleaning out, she went through her own things and added some of those into the donate boxes and rubbish bags.

She even started a little cleaning, but there was too much stacked around the place for her to make too much of a difference, so she gave up.

All of a sudden, she couldn't wait to get rid of it, so she picked up a box and took it to the Charity Shop, arranging with Karen to send a truck to collect the extra furniture as well as the boxes.

Sadly, too late to arrange for the next day, but the day after was fine.

And by too late, Summer realised she'd missed lunch, and it was mid-afternoon, so she rushed to the cafe which was getting ready to close.

The girl behind the counter, whose name was Judy, offered her a slightly overcooked lasagne at a steep discount to go with her latte.

They chatted for a while, and Judy mentioned she was competing in a poetry slam at the local pub that evening and Summer should consider going along.

Summer's inclination as she ate the lukewarm lasagne at home was not to, but she knew making friends was about making an effort, so at the last minute she bathed and changed and went to the pub.

The following day was a 1:

Today you'll plan new projects related to self-sufficiency and self-determination. Alone time may be of benefit.

She sat at her desk, working steadily to catch up with her backlog.

And as she got to lunchtime, she started to feel restless and decided to walk a donation down to chat with Karen and catch up with Judy on the way back.

Karen mentioned she needed someone to take care of some paperwork for the shop, and Summer said she was a virtual assistant and found herself with a new client.

Judy needed someone to transcribe her poems for a publication, so Summer found herself with a second client.

The next day was 6:

Today you'll focus on nurturing and supporting home, friends and family.

Summer was delighted when Karen and the van arrived early in the day, and by mid-morning, the flat was almost empty by comparison.

She opened all the windows and set to cleaning the place as if it had never been cleaned before.

Which it hadn't really.

She rearranged what was left of the furniture, and found homes for the bits and pieces she'd kept of her parents' things.

In just a few days, her flat had become a home, and she'd met a couple of people she could invite to visit.

She decided she needed some flowers to put in her mother's tall cut glass vase, but first, she visited the charity shop and invited Karen to stop by for drinks later that evening.

And then she stopped at the cafe and invited Judy.

Next stop the supermarket for snacks, the bottle shop for wine, and the florist for long-stemmed orange and yellow roses.

There was nothing to do in the flat, so she put the wine in the fridge, then put her feet up and waited for her new friends to arrive.

Secure future, new methods, and not one, but two friends.

THE END

As a small token of my thanks for reading...

Please enjoy 10% off everything (excluding shipping)

at alexandriablaelock.com

with the code summerten.

Turn the page for some ideas where to use it,

Felicia Clarke; influencer.

Old Fashioned. Fiercely independent.

Encourages others, but treads her own path.

Dead, but fondly remembered.

By some.

Meet Morag Clementine. The new housekeeper at historic Hayward Hall.

Her practical and capable attitude usually keeps her out of trouble.

bove all, her no-nonsense, get it done approach. And her get in the middle of the scrum outlook. Just as well, because Hayward Hall needs someone like her.

In this genre-spanning collection of original stories, Morag finds herself ensnared in the History of Hayward Hall...

No ordinary housekeeper, can Morag save the house, one century at a time?

Do you have what it takes to be a hero?

Whether that's running into a burning building, standing up for what you know is right, or saving the Princess it's going to take everything you've got and more besides.

In this genre-spanning collection of original stories, five women draw on resources they didn't know they had:

Join them, if you dare.

Perhaps you'll carry your new books
in one of these bags

Enjoy them while drinking from
one of these mugs

Or wearing one of these t-shirts

ABOUT THE AUTHOR

Australian author Alexandria Blaelock writes mostly fantasy and mystery.

She's appeared in the Stringybark Anthology *Crowd Surfing, Pulphouse Fiction Magazine*, and *Ellery Queen's Mystery Magazine*.

She's also written five self-help books applying business techniques to personal matters like getting dressed, tidying up, and feeding friends.

Discover more at https://alexandriablaelock.com.